COOL!

To the Foreman family

COOL!

michael morpurgo

Illustrated by

MICHAEL FOREMAN

HarperCollins *Children's Books*

First published in Great Britain by HarperCollins *Children's Books* 2002
HarperCollins *Children's Books* is a division of HarperCollins*Publishers* Ltd
77-85 Fulham Palace Road, Hammersmith, London W6 8JB

The HarperCollins *Children's Books* website address is:
www.harpercollinschildren'sbooks.co.uk

4

ISBN 0 00 713103 8

Printed and bound in England by
Clays Ltd, St Ives plc

BOY IN CAR ACCIDENT COMA

Robbie Ainsley, 10, of Tiverton was in a coma tonight in Wonford Hospital, Exeter, after being knocked down by a car outside his house. Doctors at the hospital say his condition is serious but stable. The driver, a man in his forties, is helping police with their enquiries.

1

I think a lot about Lucky, and I wish I didn't, because Lucky's dead. It makes me so sad. It was me that chose his name, too. But Lucky turned out to be not so lucky after all. I want to cry, but I can't. What's worse is I don't know why I can't cry. I just can't.

Sometimes I tell myself that maybe I'm in the middle of a bad dream, a terrible nightmare, that soon I'll wake up and Lucky will be alive and everything will be just as it was. But dreams and nightmares only end when you wake up, and I can't wake up. I try. I try all the time, but I can't. So then I know it can't be a dream, that what happened to me and to Lucky was real and true, that Lucky is dead and I'm locked inside my head and can't get out.

I can't wake up. But I *can* hear. I can feel, too. I can smell. And I can remember. I remember it all, every moment of how it happened. It was Saturday, just after breakfast. I had the whole weekend ahead of me. Footie in the park with Marty and the others. Then I'd be going out with Dad on Sunday. We'd be going sailing again at Salcombe. I couldn't wait.

The phone rang. Dad. It would be Dad. He always rang on Saturday mornings. As usual, Mum didn't pick it up at once. She just let it ring and ring. And when she did pick it up she wasn't at all friendly. It was a long time now since she'd been friendly with Dad. Lucky yapped at the phone. Lucky yapped like a puppy at just about everything – the postman, the milkman, a fly on the window, a dog on TV. He wasn't actually a puppy at all. He was even older than me. He'd just never grown up, that's all. Always busy, always bouncy.

Mum had the phone in her hand now, and I could hear Dad saying, "Hello? Hello?"

"Take him for a walk, Robbie," said Mum, ignoring Dad on the phone. "I want a word with your father." She was always 'having a word' with Dad, but they never sorted things out between them. I sat where I was because I wanted to hear what was going on. "Robbie! Do as I say. Take Lucky for a walk!" I pretended I hadn't heard her. "Robbie, *please* take that dog for a walk. All right you can get yourself an ice-cream."

"Cool," I said.

Then she got really mad. "Don't say 'cool'. You know how I hate it. Out!"

"OK. Cool," I said, just to irritate her. "Come on, Lucky. Walkies."

Ellie called out from upstairs, asking if she could come with me. I said no because she'd be ages putting on her boots, and because she always wanted to stop to feed the ducks. Lucky was jumping up and down, yapping. After all, he'd just heard the best word in the world – *walkies*. I opened the front door and Lucky shot off down the path, still yapping. We were going walkies in the park and he was loving it already.

Normally, I put Lucky's lead on and he

jumps up and down while I open our front gate. But the front gate was open already. Someone had left it open. Then I saw the cat – Mrs Chilton's big tabby cat. She was sitting on the wall in the sunshine, licking herself – on the far side of the road. It all happened so fast after that. Lucky was gone,

skittering down the path, his little legs going like crazy underneath him, growling and yapping all at the same time. And I was laughing because he looked so funny. Suddenly I stopped laughing because I saw the danger I should have seen in the first place. I shouted, but it was too late.

Lucky was out of the gate and into the road before I could stop him. I ran after him. I heard the car, heard the squeal of brakes, saw Lucky disappear underneath the wheels. But I never saw the car that hit me. I felt it though. I even heard my own scream. I was flying through the air, and falling, tumbling, rolling.

Then I was in the ambulance. But somehow I couldn't wake up. Nothing seemed to work. I couldn't move anything, not my fingers, not my legs. But *inside* my head I *had* woken up. Inside I was wide awake.

I remember thinking in the ambulance, "Maybe I'm dead. Maybe this is what being dead really feels like." I've thought a lot about that ever since, and it doesn't worry me any more, not often anyway. I know I can't be dead because my leg hurts all the time, so does my head. I feel like I've been walked all over by a herd of elephants. I mean, you can't hurt if you're dead, can you?

I could hear Mum crying, and the ambulance man telling her I would be all right, that she wasn't to worry, that it wasn't far to the hospital. I remember he put a mask over my mouth. When we got here, I felt the cold air on my face. Mum held my hand the whole time. She kept kissing me and crying, and I wanted to open my eyes and tell her I was fine. But I couldn't, and I still can't.

She's here in the room with me now, with Ellie. There were times I couldn't stand the sight of my little sister – she could be so annoying. Now I'd give anything, anything in the world, just to be able to open my eyes and see her again.

Mum and Ellie don't cry as often as they did, thank goodness. Dr Smellybreath told them that crying would only upset me, that they should talk to me, that I can hear them if they do. But from the way they talk to me, I know they don't really believe I can hear them. They just hope I can. They do try to talk to me sometimes, but mostly they talk *about* me, not to me, like they're doing now.

"He looks very pink," Ellie's saying, and she's touching my cheek. I can feel the sharpness of her little fingernail. "And he's very hot, too." She's sitting on my bed now. She's playing with my fingers like they were toys. "This little piggy went to market, this little piggy stayed at home..." She's done this before. She'll do the whole nursery rhyme including the tickling bit at the end. Here we go: "And this little piggy cried 'wee wee wee' all the way home." And she's running her tickling fingers all the way up my arm. They do tickle too, but I can't giggle like she wants me to. I want to wake up right now and tickle her back, tickle her till she bursts. I love to make her giggle. But I can't do it. I can't.

"What's Robbie got that pipe thing in his mouth for, Mum?" she asks again. And Mum explains, again, and tells her not to touch my tubes, again. "Why doesn't he wake up, Mum?"

"He will, Ellie, he will. When he's ready to, he will. He's just sleeping. He's tired."

"Why's he tired?"

Mum doesn't answer, because she can't.

There are so many questions I want to ask them. I want to ask what all my tubes are for. I'm full of horrible tubes going into me and out of me. I want to ask about Lucky. Is he really dead? Tell me. I have to know for sure, one way or the other. And also, I want to know if Chelsea won on Saturday. Did Zola score? I bet he did. Coolest player in the whole world. The best.

And another thing. How long have I been lying here in this bed? The trouble is there's no night or day for me, no yesterday, no today, no tomorrow; so it's difficult to know how long I've been here. I'm guessing it's about three days, maybe four. But I can't really be sure.

I doze a lot, but I never know for how long. I feel like dozing off right now. I 'm so sleepy. When I wake up Mum'll still be here, with Ellie, and with Gran probably – Gran's just gone off shopping. Or maybe Dad'll be here instead, or Doctor Smellybreath will be sticking something into me or pulling something out of me. Or Tracey will be with me again, making me comfortable. She's my nurse and she's really cool. She smells nice too. She smells of flowers. Not like Doctor Smellybreath. He smells of garlic.

Tracey often sings as she works. She's got favourite songs and favourite singers – John Lennon and Kirsty MacColl. She says Kirsty MacColl is just the best. She plays me the CD sometimes. Tracey tells me secrets, too. That's one really good thing

I've discovered about being in a coma; sometimes people tell me secret things. Maybe it's because they don't really believe I can hear them, that I'll ever wake up. But I can and I will. Tracey's always going on about her boyfriend, Trevor, where they went last night, what he said to her when he said goodnight. Trevor! What a name!

She was angry with him again this morning, because he forgot her birthday. Either she's furious with him or she loves him to bits. Can't make up her mind. I reckon Trevor must be a nerd, a right nerd. I'll tell her so when I wake up.

I'm dozing off now, drifting away. But Mum won't let me. She's bending over me. She's still here. She's close to me. I can feel her warmth, feel her hair falling on my face as she kisses me. "Your dad'll be in to see you later, Robbie. And I'll be in again tomorrow." Now she's crying. "Please wake up, Robbie, please."

I'm trying, Mum, I'm trying. And Ellie's kissing me too. I've got a wet ear now.

"I brought you Pongo," she says. "He'll look after you. He'll help you wake up."

Pongo is her flop-eared, cuddly rabbit, pale blue with pink eyes. He's her absolute favourite cuddly toy. She hates being without him. I want to hug her. I want to say thank you. I want to tell her that Pongo's cool, really cool. But they've gone, and I'm alone.

PRAYERS AT SCHOOL FOR COMA BOY

Prayers were said this morning at the primary school in Tiverton for Robbie Ainsley who was knocked down by a car last week. Headteacher Mrs Tinley said: "Robbie is a very popular boy at school with children and teachers alike. He plays centre forward in the school football team, sings in the choir, and only recently played Oliver Twist in our school production of Oliver."

Robbie Ainsley remains in a coma and on a life support system in Wonford Hospital where doctors say his condition is unchanged.

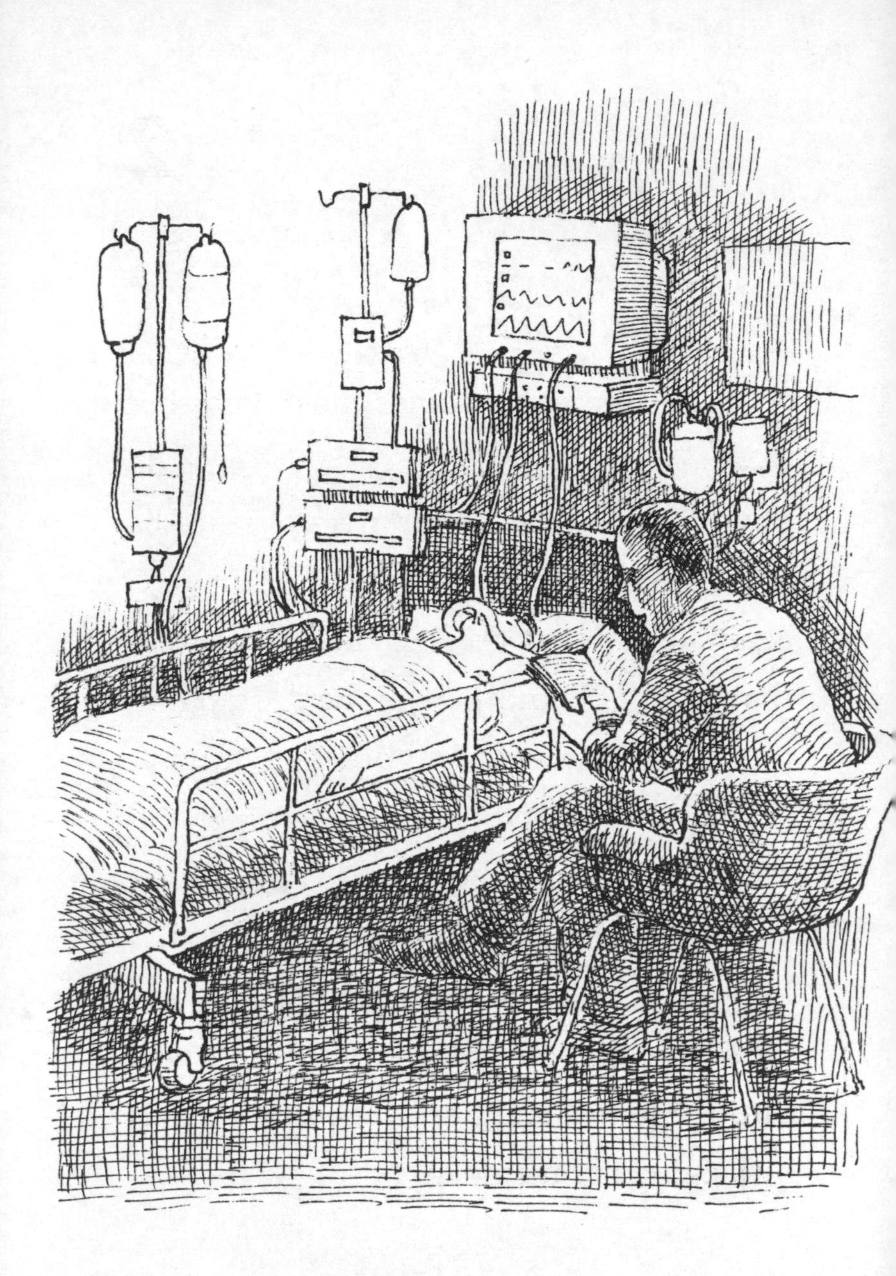

2

Dad's here. He comes most days, but never with Mum. They don't do anything together any more, not since he moved out. He's reading to me. *The BFG* again. It's always *The BFG*. I like it, but not that much. I know why he's doing it, though. Doctor Smellybreath's always saying it, to everyone who comes to visit me. He says anything could wake me up at any time – a voice I recognise, a book I know, a song I like, or some big surprise. He says everyone's got to try to find a way through to me, and one of the best ways is by jogging my memory.

So Dad sits here reading *The BFG*. I know it by heart, Dad, and it's not waking me up. Talk to me, Dad. I just want you to talk to me, like you used to. But he doesn't. He always says exactly the same thing when he first comes in to see me. "Hello, Robbie. You all right then?" Silly question, Dad. Then he gives me a kiss on my forehead, pats my hand, sits down and starts to read. He doesn't even tell me who won the football.

Sometimes he stops reading for a while and I hear him breathing, and I feel him just sitting there looking at me. He's doing that now. I know he is. He's moving his chair closer. He's going to talk to me. He's going to say something.

"Robbie? Robbie? Are you there?" Of course I am, Dad. Where else would I be?

My nose is itching, Dad. I wish you would scratch it for me. I wish I could scratch it for me.

"Say something to me, Robbie. Move a finger, or anything. Please." I can't, Dad. Don't you think I would if I could?

"I'll finish the chapter then, shall I?" He's closer still now, so close I can feel his breath on my ear. "It's *The BFG*, Robbie. Your favourite." I know it is, Dad. Please don't read to me, Dad. Just talk to me. But I hear him turning the page. On he goes. I shouldn't complain. He reads it brilliantly. Well, he should. He is an actor after all. His BFG voice is really cool, all booming and funny, like laughing thunder.

Great! Tracey's come in again. She's singing. I love to hear her singing. *Days I'll remember all my life*. Kirsty MacColl.

It makes me feel all happy and warm inside. "Hello, Mr Ainsley," she chirps. "How are we today? How's Robbie doing?"

"The same," Dad says. "Much the same. Sometimes I don't see any point in this. I don't think he knows I'm even here." I wish he wouldn't sound so gloomy.

"Don't you believe it," says Tracey. "He knows, don't you, Robbie? I know he knows, Mr Ainsley." She's changing the dressing on my head. "He knows a lot more than you think, I'm sure of it. He's doing just fine, Mr Ainsley. What he doesn't need is people around him who are worrying themselves silly about him." You tell him, Tracey. I can feel the warmth of her hands on my head. "Well, the bump on his head is going down very nicely, and that's just what we want. But it's swollen on the inside, Mr Ainsley. That's the big problem. All we need is for that swelling to go down too, and with a little bit of luck, and with a lot of encouragement, he'll come out of his coma."

"Mrs Tinley – she's Robbie's Headteacher," Dad's saying, "she gave me this tape to play for Robbie. The kids in his class have sent messages to him – you know, get-well messages. She thought it might help, help him to wake up. What d'you think?"

"I think that's really sweet," Tracey says. "And what's more it's a great idea. I'll go and find the cassette machine. We've got one somewhere, I know we have." And she goes out, leaving Dad and me alone again.

There's a bit of a silence, and then suddenly Dad starts to talk. For the first time he's actually talking as if he really believes I might be able to hear him. "Robbie, it's about your mum and me. We both feel really bad about this. She thinks that if she hadn't sent you off to walk Lucky in the park, then none of this would have happened. And I know that if I'd been at home, then I'd have been there to take you and Lucky to the park myself. I'd have been there to look after you.

And there's something else, Robbie. About your mum and me splitting up. I should have said something before, I should have explained. It was my fault, not Mum's – mostly anyway. I couldn't get work, Robbie, and I got all down in the dumps, and fed up and depressed. I thought

I wasn't any use to anyone – not her, not you, not Ellie. She had enough of me moping about the place, feeling all sorry for myself. I don't blame Mum. We both said things we shouldn't have said. Now I'm upset and she's upset."

Dad never *ever* talks to me like this. He isn't talking to me as if I'm a kid at all. I like that. I like that a lot. "I've got a job now, Robbie. It's not much, just a little part on TV, in *The Bill*. But it's something, a start. I'm getting back on my feet. I'd come home like a shot, but I think I've blown it and I don't know if Mum'll have me back."

Course she would, Dad. Ask her. She misses you like anything. We all do. Ask her, Dad. Just ask her! I want to shout it out loud. But I can't even open my mouth to talk.

Tracey's back. "Here it is," she says. "I'll plug it in, shall I? Not too loud now. Good luck." And she's gone again.

"It's your friends from school, Robbie. They all wanted to say hi. That's nice, isn't it?" All of them? I don't think so, Dad. Certainly not Barry Bolshaw, him with the big mouth, who has a go at me whenever he can, just for the fun of it. I hate his guts, and he hates mine. I can't say my 'r's very well, so he calls me 'Wobbie' or 'weedy Wobbie', just because I'm a bit on the small side.

Dad's really hopeless with machines, always has been. He keeps pressing the wrong buttons. Ah, at last. Here we go.

"Hello Robbie," Mrs Tinley's voice. "This is Mrs Tinley." Well, I know that, don't I? "Class 6c are here with lots of messages to help you feel better. First a song to cheer you up. Ready children? One. Two. Three." *"Food, glorious food..."*

They sing the whole song, and I sing along with it in my head. I know it off by heart. I can hear Marty droning along in the background. He's useless at singing. He can only sing one note, but he doesn't seem to know it, and the trouble is he always sings really loudly.

Marty's my best friend, ever since Infants. He's got sticking out ears and sticking up hair. That's the thing about

Marty – he sticks out. He's got huge great feet, like his Dad. I tried on his Dad's shoes once when I was little. Like clowns' shoes they were. I often go round to Marty's place. I love it there. No one ever tidies up, and his Mum and Dad laugh a lot, and so does Marty. Sometimes I take Lucky with me. They've got a big garden, and Lucky races around and digs in the sand pit, and they love him to bits. Marty dog-sits for us when we go away. It's like a second home for Lucky – or it was. Marty's a brilliant footballer, too – he's goalie in our school team. He's got great big hands, like spades, and the ball always seems to stick to them.

The song's over and Mrs Tinley's banging on about how much they all want me to get better. "Now, Robbie. Here's Marty with the first message."

"Hi, Rob. We played St Jude's on Saturday, and we won, of course. We hammered them 4–1. And the goal they got was a penalty, which wasn't fair – I never touched their centre forward. He dived. Get better soon because we miss having you around. And we need you back in the team, too. See ya."

"Hiya Robbie. It's Lauren. I'm the new girl who sits at the back and has coloured braids in her hair. You've got to get better soon, because we all get very sad when we think of you in hospital. Bye for now."

"Robbie, it's your *check*mate, Morris." Morris, a real boffin, the school chess champion – looks like Harry Potter – brain like a computer. I only ever beat him once, and then I cheated. Bit of a weirdo. He's always making jokes, and then explaining them as if you're stupid or something. He's doing it now. "*Check*mate. *Check*mate. Get it? *Check*mate. Come back soon, so's I can *check*mate you again. Right?"

"Hey Robbie. This is Barry. Remember me?" Not likely to forget you, am I? Barry being friendly? Barry being nice? "Listen, I just want to say get better, that's all. When you come back we could be mates, yeah?" And he sounds as if he really means it, too. Maybe he's not as bad as I thought after all.

"This is Freya. Can you hear me, Robbie?" That's Freya Porter, who's very quiet and always wears those mules – sort of clog-type shoes. I think her mother's Dutch. She speaks with a bit of an accent, but she's better at spelling than any of us. "I think what happened to you was terrible. I say prayers for you each night and hope that will help. I hope you come out of your sleep very soon."

"Imran here, Robbie." Bill Sykes in *Oliver Twist*. "You've got to open your eyes and do stuff, 'cos if you don't, you won't get to be in our next show. I just came back from my holiday in Spain when I heard about your accident, and my mum and my dad and me hope you get better very soon."

Then Sam. Then Juliet. Then Joe. *All* of them. Everyone in my class. I just want to jump out of this bed, run down the road, across the playground, into the classroom, and shout out: "Here I am! I'm back! I'm better!" But all I can do is lie here and cry inside. Now they're singing another song from *Oliver – You've got to pick a pocket or two*. I love that one. Inside I'm laughing and crying all at the same time.

"Did you hear all that, Robbie?" Dad again. "They're all rooting for you, just like all of us are, me and Mum and Ellie and Gran. Wake up, Robbie." He's shaking my shoulder now, gently. "Please, Robbie. Listen, I'll try to put things right with Mum, OK? Would you get better if I did that? I can't promise anything, but I'll try. I'll really try. Would that help?"

Yes, Dad. That would help. That'd be cool, really cool. The best. But all my words are inside my head. I want to let them out, so Dad can hear me. But somehow they can't escape.

Dad's going. He's hugging me. He's been crying. I can feel the tears on his cheeks. I wish I could cry. I wish I could cry buckets.

COMA BOY NO BETTER

Robbie Ainsley is still in a coma at Wonford Hospital in Exeter after being knocked down by a car over two weeks ago. The driver, Mr George McAllister, a forty-five year old solicitor from Dumfries in Scotland, was questioned at the time and released. Police say that no criminal charges will be brought against him. From his home, Mr McAllister today made this statement: "I deeply regret what has happened to young Robbie Ainsley. I was not speeding. I did all I could to stop. I was just in the wrong place at the wrong time. I just hope and pray that Robbie will pull through."

3

I've been having these horrible thoughts about Mum and Dad. I've had them ever since Dad left home, but they keep coming back and I can't stop them. I just can't get them out of my head. I've tried. But I keep seeing that huge collage of family photos in our front hall at home, stretching from the kitchen door to the back room. There's hundreds of pictures of all of us, going back years and years – holidays, school photos, Christmases, birthday parties – all mixed together, a sort of family patchwork, a patchwork of memories. Lucky sleeping inside my pram. Lucky swimming with me. I used to stand there in the hall when I was little, gazing up at them, usually looking for me and Lucky. Now I can see them in my head. I'm looking at them now.

There's lots of photos of Mum and Dad before they got married, before they had me. They look really young and happy, on a skiing trip together, by the sea, just having fun. There's wedding photos – Mum in a long white dress and Dad all posh in a suit. Then I'm there with them. After that they don't look quite so happy in the photos ever again. I always seem to be between them – first me, then Ellie.

Since the day Dad left us, I think I've always known it – no matter what Dad told me the other day. I know that it was *me* that split them up, me and Ellie, but mostly me I think, because I was the first. I caused the split. I made Dad leave – not on purpose, of course not, but just by being there, just by being born.

If Dad could only put things right with Mum, like he says he will, then I know I wouldn't have to have these horrible thoughts any more. I hope he can. I so hope he can. I'd cross my fingers if I could.

I doze, off and on, on and off. But I'm still here. I'm always still here, lying on my bed. People come and people go all the time. Marty pops in to see me sometimes, but he never stays long because he doesn't know what to say. He never talks about the accident. No one does. He never says a word about Lucky.

No one does. But at least he gives me the football scores. Chelsea lost on Saturday to Arsenal, and Marty was over the moon. That's the only sad thing about Marty – he's an Arsenal fan. Then Mrs Tinley brought me some flowers when she came. Mum was there. "Mrs Tinley's got you some lovely freesias, Robbie," she said. "Isn't that nice? You can talk to him if you like, Mrs Tinley." I don't think Mrs Tinley wanted to talk to me, not really. She cleared her throat. "Well Robbie. I hope you liked the tape we sent you. You'd better get back to school quick you know. You're missing a lot of lessons." I hadn't thought of that before she said it, and it made me feel like laughing. But I couldn't.

Sometimes I seem to get muddled about who was here and when, and about who's still in the room. I think Mrs Tinley must have gone, because Mum and Gran and Ellie have been here for a while now, and they're not talking as if Mrs Tinley's still here. Ellie's been moaning on about how I don't look after Pongo like I should, because she found him on the floor under the bed. And Gran keeps crying and sniffing and saying she can't help it. Mum's saying it'll be time to go soon. And I'm dozing off again.

Dad's here now. Only a short visit, he says. He has to get off to rehearsals. He's really happy. He tells me he's got another job, in panto. He's going to be one of the ugly sisters in *Cinderella* at the Northcott Theatre. "On at Christmas," he says. "You'll have to come and see me." So I've got a Dad who's an ugly sister. Weird or what?

He whispers in my ear as he's going: "I think I've got a nice surprise for you, Robbie. It'll take a bit of fixing up, but when it comes, it'll be the best surprise in the world. I promise you. Can't tell you what it is, or it won't be a surprise. The doctor says surprises are good for you, and the bigger the surprise the better. This one could really wake you up, Robbie. That's what he says. This is a whopper of a surprise. A real whopper!"

I know at once what it is. Obvious. Him and Mum, they've got together again. And that's cool. Really cool!

I've been lying here ever since he left, feeling so happy about it. But I've been thinking that Dad shouldn't have said anything to me about the 'surprise', because now I've guessed what it is, it won't be a surprise, will it? And if it isn't a surprise then it can't wake me up, can it? It hasn't worked so far. I mean, I'm still asleep inside my coma. Coma – funny word, that. Looks a bit like comma. Sounds like it, too. Hope my coma is a comma, and not a full stop. I'm not exactly frightened of the "full stop". But I would miss everyone, everyone at home, Marty, Chelsea, Zola. I'd miss Zola a whole lot.

Anyway, it'll be great for Ellie if Mum and Dad have got back together again. When Dad left she was always coming into my room and crying her eyes out, and there was nothing I could do or say to make her feel any better. So even if my coma does turn out to be a "full stop" and I don't wake up, at least Ellie will be happy again. That'd be cool. Don't know why Mum hates me saying that so much. 'Cool' is really cool!

Tracey says it a lot too. She said it just a moment ago when she came in to give me my bedbath. My best time of the day. I get to feel so fed up sometimes, and then Tracey comes in and she's always happy and cheerful and chatty. "Bedbath, Robbie. Oh, look at the lovely flowers someone's brought you! Here, smell." And she wafts them under my nose. "Freesias. The best. Really cool. I only like flowers that smell nice. Don't see any point in flowers if they don't smell. So Robbie, I hear you've got an ugly sister for a Dad. He was telling me that what he wants most in all the world now is for you to come and see him in the panto at

Christmas. That gives you just five weeks to wake your ideas up and get yourself out of here. Not that I want to see you go. You're good company. You know what I like about you, Robbie? You never complain. But then I suppose you're the one patient I want to complain. The day you wake up and complain, you'll be on your way out of here, and that'll make everyone really happy, especially me."

She chats on and on all the way through my bedbath. "By the way, Robbie, your Mum rang up. She's coming in to see you again this evening, and she's bringing someone else with her. She didn't say who. Your Gran, I suppose. She's lovely, your Gran."

Please not Gran again. She'll only sniffle. I mean, I love her lots. She's the coolest Gran anyone could ever have, a real wizard on computer games and she makes great pancakes, but she sniffles and she smells all powdery when she kisses me. And she's been kissing me quite a lot lately. Everyone has, except Tracey. And I sort of wish she would. I like Tracey. I mean I get fed up hearing about all her troubles with Trevor the nerd, and all about her diet; but at least she talks to me like I'm listening, like I'm really alive, like I'm going to stay alive.

"There, that's your bedbath done," Tracey says. "That should make you feel a little better." And she's gone. I want so much to thank her. Because I do feel better. I feel fresher now, not sticky any more, not so manky. And anyway, I always feel better when Tracey's around. From her voice I've made up a picture of her in my head. She's about thirty and she sounds very pretty. She's tall, I reckon, and she's got dark hair. And she has a nose ring. I don't know why, but I'm sure she's got a nose ring. I'll see for myself one day, see how right or wrong I was. Not that it matters. She's cool, anyway.

Mum's come in again, like Tracey said she would. But Gran's not with her. No powdery kiss. There's someone else. "Robbie, I've brought someone in to see you. It's all right, Mr McAllister. You can talk to Robbie, he'll hear you."

"Robbie? Robbie?" Not a voice I know, not a name I know. "I just had to come to say how sorry I am. My name's Ian, Ian McAllister. It was me that knocked you down. Ever since it happened I've been wanting to tell you, to explain... just to say how terrible I feel. And then your Mum rang me, and said it might help if I came to see you."

You feel terrible. How do you think *I* feel? "It all happened so quickly. One moment there was your dog running out into the road, and that other car hit it. And then you were there, right in front of me. I saw you too late, Robbie. I tried to stop. I really did... I'm sorry. I'm so sorry." He sounds Scottish, and he sounds upset, too, really unhappy.

"Robbie, Mr McAllister has come all the way down from Scotland to see you." What do you want me to do, Mum? Do you want me to dance a Highland fling? Do you want me to wake up and say thank you? OK. Thanks for running me over, Mr McThingemejig. I'm so angry. I'm churning up inside. I'm thinking: if you hadn't been driving along in your silly car when I ran out, then I wouldn't be here, would I? I mean, what are brakes for, Mr McThingemejig?

"Robbie, if I could turn the clock back..." He's taking my hand. He sounds as if he's got a moustache and a very short haircut. He sounds kind too, and honest. He's saying what he feels, and suddenly I'm not so angry with him any more. "I've got kids of my own, Robbie, a bit older than you. And do you know what? I don't even dare tell them about what I've done. Back home I can't look folk in the eye any more." He's not crying exactly, but his voice is very wobbly.

"I didn't know what to bring you. But your Mum told me how you love your football. So I've brought you a footie for when you get better. OK? Just you get better now, Robbie, so's you can wake up and give it a right good kicking. And you can maybe give me a right good kicking and all, for putting you where you are now. How'd that be?" Cool, I'm thinking. He's patting my hand. "I'm off now. See you, Robbie."

Mum's showing him out. "Thanks for coming," she's saying.

"Listen, Mrs Ainsley. I'd do anything, anything at all to help. And thanks, thanks for letting me come. I feel so terrible about this."

"It was an accident, a dreadful accident. No one's fault. The police said you were driving slowly and safely. It just happened. All that matters now is to get Robbie better, and your coming here might just help bring him round. Anything to stir him up, to make him angry, that's what the doctors told me. And thanks for the football."

He's gone, and now I'm alone with Mum again. She's come to sit beside me. She's upset at me for not waking up. "Please Robbie, for God's sake. For my sake. Be angry. Be angry at him. Be angry at me for making you take Lucky out for his walk. Shout at me, I won't mind. Just say something. Say 'cool' if you like. Shout it out a thousand times and I won't mind. I won't ever mind again, I promise." She's crying and I want to wake up so she'll stop. I don't want to shout at her, I want to wake up and hug her.

I reckon I've had half a dozen doctors in to see me, all looking after different bits of me – my head, my brain, my leg. But mostly I have Dr Smellybreath. He's here now, pulling back my eyelids and breathing his garlicky breath all over me. Mum keeps asking him questions which he doesn't want to answer. "Is there any change, Doctor?" "What about brain damage?" "Has the swelling inside gone down, d'you think?" "Doctor, how long can he just lie there like this?" When Dr Smellybreath finishes all his poking and prodding, they go outside together, so I never hear the answers. It's *me* you're talking about, you know. Me – *my* head, *my* brain, *my* life. Don't I have a right to know what's going on?

In between my dozings off, all I can think about is Dad's big surprise. Mum never let on anything about it. But that's cool. She wouldn't, would she? After all, it's a secret, isn't it?

Tracey's come bouncing in. "All alone are we, Robbie?" She's bending over me. "I've got news for you," she whispers. "You're the first person I've told. See this, Robbie?" Silly question, Tracey. Course

I can't. "My ring. Just a cheap ring for now – we'll get a proper one later. Trevor. He's only asked me to marry him! Isn't that great? Isn't that cool?"

Cool, Tracey. Yeah, really cool.

ROBBIE STILL FIGHTING FOR LIFE

A month ago today Robbie Ainsley was knocked down by a car outside his home in Tiverton. He suffered serious head injuries and a broken leg and has been in a coma and on a life support system at Wonford Hospital ever since. Doctors say that the longer he remains in a coma the less likely he is to make a full recovery. His mother, Mrs Jenny Ainsley, said today: "Robbie's fighting to stay with us. The doctors and nurses are doing all they can. And we, his family and friends, are all praying and hoping. We have to believe the best. We have to believe he'll come through this."

4

Dad seems to have forgotten all about that big 'surprise' of his. I've been looking forward to it happening every day, longing for it, but each time Mum and Dad come to see me, they come in separately. Mum doesn't talk about Dad. Dad doesn't talk about Mum. Nothing changes. Dad's always promising things. I don't know why I ever believe him. Neither of them ever says a word about Lucky. But then if he's dead, why would they? They'd know it would only upset me.

Ellie thinks I'm half-dead already. She keeps asking Mum if I'll go to heaven when I'm dead. There'd better be football in heaven, that's all I can say. If I'm going to be dead, I want there to be a heaven. But I don't want to go there yet, or anywhere else. I want to stay here, and I want to stay alive. I know that if I want to stay alive, I've got to wake myself up. I must. I try really hard to break out, but my mind just won't let me. It's like it's locked from the outside and I can't find the key.

It's funny. Before the accident I used to love dreaming. I can remember knowing I was in a dream and trying not to wake up from it, trying all I could to stay inside my dream to find out where it would take me, what would happen in the end. But I'd always wake up before I wanted to, so I'd never find out how my dream ended. Now, all I want is to get out of my dream – that's what I'm in, a sort of dream-bubble that I know is real. I so want it to burst, for me to break free, live properly, be me again. Instead, I just lie here like a great vegetable, wired up to machines that keep me alive. All I do is exist.

There's a strange sort of buzz about the hospital today. Everyone's whispering instead of talking. It's like they're trying to keep something from me. Even Tracey's gone all mysterious on me. She's giving me an especially long bedbath. "I'm not saying a word, Robbie, not a word, not if you opened your eyes this minute. If you offered me a million quid, you wouldn't get it out of me. No way José!" Now she's singing that song again: "*Days I'll remember all my life…* and this is your great day, Robbie. I want you to look your very best for your great day." What great day? What is she going on about? Am I leaving hospital? What do they know that I don't?

I can hear lots of giggling going on outside, then lots of shushing. Now the door's opening. It squeaks and clunks, which is lucky for me because I can always tell when someone's just come in or just gone out. That door's been squeaking and clunking a lot more than usual in the last couple of hours.

"Hello Robbie. You all right, then?" Dad. Dad sounding excited, but trying to hide it. He's coming nearer. "Robbie, you remember that surprise I told you about? Well, today's the day. It's here. Or rather he's here. You're not going to believe this, Robbie. But he's come to see you specially, because he's heard all about you and he wants to help you to get better. All the way from Chelsea Football Club, Robbie. It's your hero. It's Zola. Number 25. Gianfranco Zola."

"Robbie?" It's *his* voice. I recognise his Italian accent. I've heard it on TV. It's him! It's really him! It's Gianfranco Zola, the coolest footballer in the world, and he's come to see me! "Hey, Robbie. It's me. It's Gianfranco. It's like your Papa says. I came to see you, because I want you to wake up. You want to wake up for your Mama and Papa, Robbie! You want to wake up for me? You want to do this for me?"

Do I? Do I? Of course I do. I'm screaming inside, screaming with excitement, screaming to wake up. Zola! No 25! God! Right here. So close I could reach out and touch him. I want to open my eyes and see him more than anything else in the whole world.

And I should be able to do it, because this is a real surprise. So if the doctor's right, I should be waking up. But I haven't.

The truth is – and I can hardly believe I'm even thinking this – but the truth is I'm a little disappointed. I'm disappointed because this isn't the surprise I've been expecting, or hoping for. I was hoping that Mum and Dad would be coming to see me together, that Dad had moved back home and that he'd be staying. This is just silly. I've got Gianfranco Zola in my room, my absolute hero of all time, and I'm feeling let down.

I hear the chair by my bed move nearer. He's sitting down. He's taking my hand. "Your Papa, he wrote to me, Robbie. He says, please come to see my boy. So I am here. Listen. If you don't get better, you can't come back to Chelsea and see us, can you? You want to see us again, eh? 'Course you do. I'll tell you what I'll do. I'll keep a seat, especially for you, in the Directors' Box when you wake up. You like that? Next month, it's the big match. We play Manchester United at home, at Stamford Bridge. You want to be there? We'll wipe the floor with them. We'll play them off the park. We'll do it just for you. But first you've got to wake up. Do it for us, Robbie. You want us to beat Man U, OK? You've got to be there to help us. You hear me?" I hear you, Zola, I hear you. And I'm going to be there, I promise.

"And after we beat them out of sight, I tell you what we'll do, Robbie. You and me, we'll go out on the pitch and we'll kick a ball about. And I'll teach you a few tricks. How's that?

"I've got to go now. I've got training. I never miss my training. But I think about you all the time, and you think about me. OK?" He's getting up. He's going. Wake up! Say thank you! Say goodbye! Don't just lie there. "Oh, Robbie, I forgot something." He's coming back. "I've brought you a shirt. It's not from the Megastore. Nothing like that. It's my shirt, my Number 25 shirt. I wore it last week when we played West Ham. We should have won but we got lazy in the second half. Still, a draw is not too bad. And don't you worry. It's all washed nice and clean for you. Not smelly."

He's laying it over me. I can feel its softness. I can feel its blueness. I can feel the magic of it soaking into me. "It suits

you just fine, Robbie. You and me, we're both little people. But it's not about size, is it? It's about what goes on in your head. When I was a boy, maybe your age, I was always the smallest one. They told me: Gianfranco, you'll never be a footballer. You're too small, too weak. I thought inside my head, I'll show you. I'll show everyone. So. You show me, Robbie, you show everyone. You wake up. I'll look for you in the stand when we play Man U. So you'd better be there, OK?"

Then he's saying goodbye to Dad and this time he's gone for good, and I'm filling up with sadness, overflowing, bursting with it. It's like that song Mum's always playing on her Buddy Holly CD at home. *It's raining, raining in my heart.*

I can feel somehow that there's lots of people in the room now. I thought before that it was just Zola and Dad and me.

"Don't worry, Mr Ainsley. These things sometimes take time." Dr Smellybreath is examining me as he talks. "His pulse is up. So is his blood pressure. He was listening. He was hearing. I'm sure he was. We just have to give him time."

"How much time, Doctor?" Dad's saying. "How much time has he got?"

"Who knows? I've known patients live for months like this."

"But some of them don't come out of it, do they, Doctor?"

"You mustn't think like that, Mr Ainsley," Tracey's saying. "Robbie's doing his best. So are you. So are we. If we don't believe he'll come out of it, then he'll know it. If we give up on him, Mr Ainsley, he could give up on us."

"I don't know what more I can do," Dad says. "I really thought Zola would do the trick. I really did." I think he's sadder than I've ever known him.

"Listen." Tracey's speaking almost in a whisper now. But I can hear. "If Zola can't bring him back to us – and he still might –

then there'll be another way. We'll just have to find it, that's all."

"What d'you mean?"

"Let's talk about it outside, shall we? I don't think we should be talking like this in front of Robbie. He could be hearing every word we say."

The room's emptying. Everyone's going out. "That Zola," Tracey's saying as she goes, "he's dishy. He's really dishy." Then the door's squeaking and clunking and I'm alone again.

Dishy! Dishy! That man is only the best, only the coolest. And I've got his Number 25 shirt, his very own shirt. I wish Tracey would put it on me. I want to wear it. It'll be the magic I need to bring me out of myself and back to the land of the living. I know it. It's just got to be.

ZOLA IN MERCY DASH TO SAVE ROBBIE

Lying in a coma, 10-year-old accident victim Robbie Ainsley had a visit today from his great hero, Chelsea and Italy superstar, Gianfranco Zola. Zola said afterwards: "When I heard about Robbie, that he might wake up from his coma if I came to see him, I didn't have to think about it. I came to do what I can. I am a father too."

Sadly, the visit does not yet seem to have had any effect on Robbie. Doctors at Wonford Hospital say that his condition remains unchanged.

ZOLA
25

5

It's weird, but I think that maybe I've got a sort of mind-mail communication going with Tracey. Telepathy, I think it's called. Anyway, whatever it's called, it works. I've done it a few times now and I think it's really working. One moment I'm thinking something, and the next she's talking about it. It's like I can almost make her think things. Is that cool or what?

This morning I had definite proof of it. After Dr Smellybreath had examined me – again – he said something to Tracey over by the door, where he thought I couldn't hear, something I can't put out of my mind. He said: "Robbie's not looking good this morning, Tracey, not good at all. I'm beginning to think we may lose him." Lose me? *Lose* me? I was thinking… Who does old Smellybreath think he is? I'm not going to die. I'll show him. Like Zola said, I'll show him. I'll show all of them. The doctor was feeling my forehead. "How long is it exactly?" he said. "How long's he been with us?"

"Six weeks tomorrow," said Tracey. "But he's still fighting, Doctor. I know he is. He wants to come out of it so badly. And he will. I know he will. It's funny, doctor – of course he's never spoken a word to me – but sometimes I feel I really *know* Robbie, know what he's thinking. And I just know he's determined to live."

"Well, I'll be back to see him later," said

Dr Smellybreath as he went out, leaving the door squeaking and clunking behind him.

"Bed bath for you, Robbie," said Tracey.

I was almost sure this mind-mail communication thing was really real, that I wasn't inventing it, but I decided I'd put it to the test. I lay there forcing myself to think about one thing and one thing only. I focused my mind entirely on Zola's shirt. Inside my head I said to her: "Tracey, I want you to put it on me. I want to wear it. Ever since Zola came to see me and gave me his number 25 shirt I've wanted to wear it. It'll bring me luck. I know it will. Put it on me, Tracey. I want to feel its magic." And that's all I thought of as Tracey was giving me my bedbath. "Put the shirt on me, Tracey. Please. *Please*." I tried not to listen to anything she was saying, tried to close my ears, to shut out her voice. Zola's shirt. Zola's shirt. Number 25. Chelsea Blue. Chelsea 1, Arsenal 1. It's the shirt he wore against West Ham. I pictured me in it. I pictured Zola in it, and those were the pictures I kept trying to send into Tracey's mind.

At first it didn't seem to work. No matter how hard I tried I just could not make her understand. So in the end I gave up trying altogether. I'd been kidding myself all along. Of course I couldn't make contact. Vegetables can't communicate, and I'm a vegetable, nothing but a lousy vegetable. I was feeling very angry with myself for ever believing that such a thing was even possible.

She was brushing my hair and arranging my pillows when she suddenly said it.

"I know what you want, Robbie. You want your Zola shirt on, don't you? You want to wear it. I've hung it up on the back of the door so it would be the very first thing you see when you wake up. But I think you're trying to tell me you want to wear it. All right, if that's what you want, Robbie. It's your shirt. It'll be a bit big, mind, but who cares?"

It took her a while to wriggle me out of my hospital gown and into my Chelsea shirt. She was right. It was big for me, big and loose and lovely. I lay there basking in my bed in Zola's Number 25 shirt. And then Tracey said: "Hey Robbie, you look cool, really cool. And you look happy too." And I was. I am. Not only because I'm wearing his shirt, my shirt, but because I told her what I wanted her to hear, and she heard it. I had passed a mind-mail message from me to her and she had received it! I don't feel alone any more, and it's the greatest feeling in the world.

Dad's just come in. "Hello Robbie. You all right, then?" Same old Dad. But when he kisses me, I know it isn't the same old Dad at all. It's someone else, someone softer who smells a lot like Mum. It *is* Mum! It's her! They've come. Mum, Dad, they're both here, together! I wonder if Ellie is there too, but she isn't. There's no one leaping on the bed, no wet licky kiss in my ear. I miss that. I like her being here. She makes me laugh inside. But this is cool. I've got Mum and Dad together again. Maybe it took me being knocked down and Lucky being killed to bring them together, but between us we did it.

The funny thing is that no one's saying a word. Not me, not them. Then Dad's whispering to Mum, "You first. You tell him."

"No, you." And suddenly I have this horrible thought in my head. Maybe they've come here to tell me the worst news, that they've decided it's not worth keeping me alive any longer. They're going to unplug me from my life support system, and let me drift away and die. I've seen it on TV, when someone's been in a coma for ages and ages, and they just make up their minds that there's no point in going on any more. They just flick the switch and that's that.

"Robbie?" It's Mum, and she's sounding so solemn, and serious, and sad. Don't say it, Mum. Please, I'm fine inside here.

I'm going to wake up. Just give me time. Don't do it, Mum.

"Robbie, your Dad and me have been talking."

Oh God! Please, Mum. Can't you be like Tracey? Can't you read my thoughts? *I want to live, Mum. I want to stay with you. Please.*

"Well, it's like this, Robbie. Your Dad and me, we've decided… we've decided to try again – you know, being together like we were. Only not like we were. Better. Happier. We've made a mess of things, we know that, and we know how much that's upset you, upset Ellie. It upset us, too. But that's all over now."

They're not going to switch me off! They're not going to give up on me! I feel as if I'm swimming in deep warm water up towards the light, up towards the air.

But I can't reach the light. I can't breathe the air. Dad's holding one of my hands, Mum's got the other. They're trying to pull me up and out, trying to save me from drowning, willing me to break free. But something's still holding me back.

"Robbie, are you hearing this?" Dad this time. "It's you that's done this, Robbie, you and Lucky and all that's happened to you. You made us stop and think. When I've been in here with you sometimes, I could really feel you wanting us all to be together again. And Mum says she's felt just the same. So we're going to try – for us, for you, for Ellie. We're going to do our very best to make it work, Robbie. Only we want you with us. We want you to be here with us, Robbie, to come home."

Me too, Dad, me too.

"Your Dad moved back home yesterday, Robbie," Mum's saying. "So far so good." And they were both laughing like they used to do when Lucky did his party tricks, and I can hear they're easy together again, and happy.

So I should be happy too, shouldn't I? Gianfranco Zola has been in to see me and he's given me the shirt off his back – sort of. And Mum and Dad are back together. What more could I possibly want? I have this picture in my head of all of us out in the garden together, and Lucky's rolling over and over and bowing to the queen, and standing up on his little hind legs and they're all laughing and Ellie's giggling her head off.

But then I'm suddenly sad because I know Lucky is gone and will never come back. It was Lucky that always made us all laugh. I remember how I was laughing myself silly when he went skittering off after that cat, before I noticed the front gate was open, before he went under the car.

He had two black eyes like a panda, and a stubby little tail that never stopped wagging, and I loved him. We all did. He was our clown, our joker, and he was our best friend. Marty and everyone thought he was the coolest dog around, even when he came to the park and spoilt our football game, chasing after the ball, biting it, snarling at it. And when we shouted at him, he'd go running off all smiley and panting and tongue-hanging-happy. I should have put the lead on him. I should have remembered. He was dead and it was my fault.

The house would be so quiet without Lucky. Who would bite the post when it came through the door? Who would go mad and chase his tail when the telephone rang? Who would dig up Mum's flowers and send her potty? Even if I did wake up, things would never be the same without Lucky. I'm lying here with so many of my dreams come true, and yet so sad inside, as sad as I've ever been.

"That shirt suits you," says Dad. "Like Zola said, it really suits you. Wasn't he the best, coming to see you like that? It's been in all the papers, you know. Picture of him. Picture of you. I'll keep them for you, for when you come home, all right?" They're whispering together again. I can hear Mum crying and Dad's holding her, trying to comfort her. I know he is.

They're going out and I wish they wouldn't. I'm trying to call out to them to come back. But no sound comes out. The door's squeaking and clunking. They've gone. And I'm alone. I hate being left alone. I hate it.

Tracey comes in. She's singing again. It's her other song – *Imagine*. John Lennon. She's a big John Lennon fan. So's Dad. "*Imagine all the people...*" And she sings it all the way through really well. She could be a popstar, but I'm glad she's not, otherwise she wouldn't be here and I wouldn't be able to send her my mind-mail messages. I'm telling her now about Mum and Dad.

"Nice to see your mum and dad together," she says. She's hearing me, she's really hearing me! She's closing the curtains now. "Nasty out there. Raining." And then she comes and sits on my bed. "You hang in there for me, Robbie. You can do it. I know you can. I'm going off duty now. I've got a date with Trevor, and tomorrow we're going to look for a flat. He makes me really happy, you know – *and* he likes John Lennon. I'll see you the day after, right? Stay cool. See you."

And I'm thinking: Will you, Tracey? Will you? I'm not so sure. Maybe I'll be dead by then. I am so tired, Tracey. I'm tired of living like this, half alive, half dead. Maybe dying won't be so bad. Maybe I'll get to see Lucky again. I really hope so.

FEARS FOR COMA BOY

Fears for the life of 10-year-old Robbie Ainsley were growing last night as his condition was reported to have worsened. Robbie has been on a life support system in Wonford Hospital since his accident over six weeks ago. Despite all efforts to revive him, doctors say Robbie is still in a deep coma. They are still hopeful of recovery, but they point out that the longer Robbie stays in a coma the less likely this is. His family are almost constantly at his bedside, and prayers were being said for Robbie today at the parish church in Tiverton where Robbie sings in the choir.

Doctors would not comment today as to how long they would keep Robbie alive on his life support system.

25

6

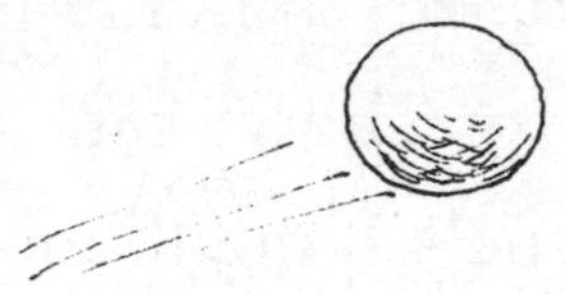

It's strange, but lately people have almost stopped talking to me – except Ellie of course who never stops talking anyway. But they never let her stay for long. Tracey or Gran or someone always takes her outside to play because she's making too much noise. I wish they wouldn't, because at least she's giggly and happy, and I like her noise. It's normal. No one else is normal, not any more.

Marty tries to talk, tries to be cheerful, but he's not very good at pretending. He can't keep it up for long. He's never got used to seeing me like this, I think. It still upsets him. I try to send him my mind-mail messages, but somehow I can't reach him. And I reckon he's lying to me, too. Just lately, almost every time he comes in, he tells me Chelsea have won another match – second in the league now, he says. Well, Chelsea never win all their matches, they're up and down like yo-yos. He's just trying to make me feel better. He put his hand on mine last time he came and squeezed it and told me to wake up. Then he cried and went out. First time he's touched me. I miss him. I miss football. I miss school. I miss everything.

Mum and Dad hardly say a word any more. I think they might be giving up on me. They just sit and wait, their silence and their sadness filling the air around me. They talk in occasional whispers to each other, but not so much to me as they did. Still, at least they're together. That's something. No, that's more than something. That's a whole lot.

Worst of all though, even Tracey seems to be losing heart. She doesn't sing like she used to, and she was crying when she came in a moment ago. Somehow I know she wasn't crying because of Trevor. And I'm pleased about that. I'd rather she cried over me than him. Let's face it, Robbie, if Tracey thinks you're not going to make it, then things are not looking good, not good at all.

I sleep a lot, almost all the time now. I want to stay awake in my head. I know I must, or else I'll die. I mean you can't die if you're awake, can you? It's like when you're drowning – I've read about it in books – if you want to keep afloat, if you want to keep alive, you have to stay awake. I sing Tracey's songs in my head over and over again – *Days* and *Imagine*. I know them by heart. Got to keep my mind awake. Got to keep living. But the trouble is that sleep is warm and gentle and inviting, and when it takes me by the hand I just want to go...

What's beyond sleep, I wonder? A black hole? Or Nothing? Or Heaven? I don't fancy a black hole. I certainly don't fancy nothing. I'd prefer heaven, just so long as it's not like where the Telly Tubbies live, with all those silly rabbits hopping about and that goo-goo grinning baby gurgling out of the sun. But I don't like thinking about all that. I won't think about all that. No more black holes, no more bunny-hopping heavens. Because I'm not going anywhere. I'm staying here in this bed and I'm staying alive.

I'm going to think of Chelsea against Man U and me in the Directors' Box at Stamford Bridge – that's heaven! And Zola looking up at me and giving me a great big Italian pizza of a grin and a thumbs-up, before he dribbles the ball past the Man U defenders and whacks it in the back of the net. And I'm on my feet and punching the air. Keep punching the air, Robbie. Keep cheering. Keep breathing.

"Live Robbie, live." It's not me thinking any more. It's Mum talking to me and she's squeezing my hand, trying to make me feel her, trying to make me feel anything. "Live, Robbie darling. Don't give up. Please."

I'm not giving up, Mum. It's you lot that's giving up, not me. I'm still here. I can feel you. As long as I can feel you, I'm alive. I'm sending you my mind-mail messages all the time, but you're just not listening. No one's listening any more, no one's hearing, not even Tracey.

Then Dad's getting up. "I won't be long, Robbie. The sun's streaming through the window. Bit stuffy in here. I've got to get some fresh air."

When he's gone, Mum cries quietly and holds my hand. Then she says: "Still, there's one good thing that's come out of all this, Robbie. At least you've stopped biting your nails." She's laughing. That's better, Mum. I love to hear you laughing.

"If you wake up, Robbie, there's so many things I'll never tell you off for again. I promise. I'll never say, stop biting your nails, Robbie. I'll never say, tidy your room, Robbie. I'll never say, turn off the TV. And I'll never say, stop saying 'cool'. *Promise.*"

I want so much to go on listening to her because I can hear she's smiling as she's talking and I love to hear her smiling. But I can't stay awake. I'm feeling so heavy inside, so warm. I'm falling away from her into my sleep. I can't stop myself. I can't feel her hand any more. I can't hear her voice. I try to come back to her, but I can't. I hope she'll be there when I wake up. I hope I will wake up.

Sometimes it's so difficult for me to know whether I'm dreaming or whether

I'm awake. I seem to slip into sleep, and in and out of my dreams so easily. Right now, though, I know I'm dreaming, and I want this dream to go on and on, because I'm back at home in the garden playing with Lucky. I've had this dream before and I love it. I'm lying on my back in the grass, and Lucky's standing on my chest and licking my face all over. I can't stop myself giggling and I'm trying to push him off. Now he's snuffling in my ear and whining and whimpering. His nose is cold. He smells of dog. He smells of Lucky and his breath stinks even worse than Dr Smellybreath's. I want to stay inside this dream for ever and ever. I don't want to wake up and be in hospital again. I want to stay here in the garden with Lucky.

I can hear Dad's voice, and can't make out if he's inside my dream or out of it. "Poor old Lucky," he's saying. "I'd forgotten to leave the car window open. Panting like crazy he was. Sun blazing down. No air. I was just giving him a little walk..."

Mum's interrupting. "You can't bring him up here. What if—"

And Dad says. "Look, I had to try. We've tried everything else, haven't we? I don't know why we didn't think of it before. If anything or anyone can wake Robbie up, it'll be Lucky, won't it?"

"But what if someone sees? You're not allowed dogs in hospitals."

"But no one did see. I smuggled him in under my jacket."

This is not my dream, not any more. In the garden I was in my dream. But now

I'm in hospital, and it's Dad's real voice I'm hearing. It's Lucky's real nose in my ear-hole. He's on my bed. He's licking my face as if he's cleaning up his dog bowl after a meal. He's licking every bit of my face, my eyes, my nose, my hair, my chin, my neck, my mouth. It's Lucky! He's not dead! He's here now, in the hospital, on my bed. He's alive!

But I saw him go under that car. I know I did. So he can't be alive, can he? Maybe this is still a dream after all. Only one way to find out. Only one way to be really, really certain. He's licking my eyes. He's telling me to open them. So I will. Open them, Robbie, open your eyes. Just do it. *And I do. I can. I'm seeing, and I'm seeing Lucky. It's him! It's really him.* I'm not dreaming him. His little eyes are looking right into mine. He's grinning down at me. His tongue's all dribbly. His dribble's real. *He's* real. It's all real.

I lift up my hand to stroke him, and that's when they go bananas, loopy, mad, both Mum and Dad together. "Look! He's moved his hand!" Mum's grabbed Dad by his arm.

"His eyes are open. Robbie? Robbie? Can you hear us?" "Can you see us? Talk to us Robbie. Talk to us." I'm trying to smile, and it must be working, because now they're both hugging me at once and they're both crying.

Lucky's jumped off the bed and he's yapping like crazy, and then everyone comes running in – a doctor in a white coat, who I suppose is Dr Smellybreath, and a nurse – Tracey – it has to be Tracey. I got her all wrong. She's not tall like I thought she was. She's really little, and she's blonde, and she hasn't got a nose ring. Ellie's come and climbed up on the bed. So I get more wet kisses, more hugs. I'm drowning in tears and wet kisses.

I'm trying to talk. I've only got a thin small squeaky voice, but it's mine and it works, just about. I so want to say something, but I can't get proper words out. They're all listening, waiting, and all I can do is gurgle and squeak.

"Don't try to talk, Robbie," Tracey is saying. "You're all right. You're back with us. You're fine."

"Your eyes are open, Robbie," says Ellie. "You've been sleeping for days and days and now you're awake. Look, I gave you Pongo," – she's holding up Pongo by his ears – "but I only really lent him to you till you were better. And now you're better, I can have him back, can't I?" That's my Ellie!

Dr Smellybreath is bending over me, peering at me, looking deep into my eyes with his light, then feeling my forehead. "Wonderful," he's saying. "The power of the human body to heal itself. Just amazing. Nice to have you back with us, Robbie. You had us quite worried for a while there." *You* were worried! Everyone's hugging everyone and Lucky's still going mad. A very angry looking lady in a white coat comes in and says: "What *is* going on in here? What's that dog doing on my ward?"

"That's not a dog," says Tracey, and she's laughing through her tears, "that's Lucky, and he works miracles." Then everyone's laughing and crying at the same time. I don't think I've ever made people happier. I don't think I've ever been happier myself.

Dad's the only one who hasn't said anything yet. I think, like me, that maybe he's trying to find his voice. When he does say something, it's about what I expect. "Hello, Robbie. You all right then, are you?"

"Cool, Dad," I hear myself say. "Just cool." Lucky's back up on the bed and licking himself in embarrassing places, as usual, as if nothing at all has happened.

"That dog is disgusting," says Mum.

And I say: "That dog is cool."

And Mum says: "Cool. It's such a lovely word. It's the best word in the world, the coolest."

Maybe Lucky does know what he's done, because he's looking at me now as if he's very pleased with himself, very pleased indeed. And he's smiling. The whole world's smiling.

MIRACLE BOY ROBBIE'S GREAT DAY

FOOTBALL STAR GIANFRANCO ZOLA FULFILS HIS PROMISE

In a bid to wake accident victim, 10-year-old Robbie Ainsley, from his coma, Zola promised him a VIP seat in the Directors' Box when Chelsea next played Manchester United at home. And on Saturday Robbie was there to watch his hero put Man U to the sword, and score the winning goal himself…

"It was great that Robbie was here to see us win," said the Italian star. "It wouldn't have been so good to wake up from his coma and come and see us lose, would it? I gave him a bit of a wave when I scored my goal. I dedicated that goal specially to him. It's a great day for me, for all of us at Chelsea because it's like Robbie came back from the dead almost to be with us. That's a whole lot more important than beating Manchester United, I think."

Robbie's family came along for the match as well, with the family dog, Lucky. He was knocked down in the same accident, but like Robbie he survived – *luckily*.

And Robbie's comment on his great day at Chelsea? "Gianfranco and me kicked a ball about afterwards. Just him and me – and Lucky. It was cool."

But that wasn't the end of Robbie's great day out. He was back in Exeter in time for the evening performance of the Panto at the Northcott Theatre to see his dad play the part of one of the ugly sisters.

Said Robbie: "He was cool, really cool."

I was faster than all the kids twice my age. And somehow I could always make a football do whatever I wanted it to. It just came easy to me, I don't know why, but it did.

The only thing Billy ever wanted to do was to play for Chelsea. His dream came true when he was picked for the team – but that was 1939, and the Second World War began, and then Billy's life, like everyone else's, was changed for ever.

Billy's no kid now – he's eighty today. But he's got memories, such memories…

"… told with all the author's open-hearted clarity, and richly illustrated by Michael Foreman." *Philip Pullman*

HarperCollins *Children's Books*

TORO! TORO!

**I didn't tell Paco what I'd seen that day –
I didn't ever want him to know. "It'll be soon," I told him.
"I'll take you away so you can live wild up in the hills,
where you'll be safe for ever and ever.
I'll work something out, I promise you."**

Antonio lives an idyllic life on his parents' bull farm in Andalucia, Spain. But the idyll is shattered when he realises that his beloved bull calf, Paco, is destined for the bloody struggle of the bullring. What can he do? He has a plan – a plan of such daring, it will take enormous courage to see it through.

But it is 1936, and the rolling drums of war are echoing across the Spanish plains. Little does Antonito realise the full consequences of his actions – and Paco has a destiny far exceeding Antonito's dreams.

In Toro! Toro! Michael Morpurgo unpicks the problem of taking sides, of how enemies can be good, of guilty secrets kept for years… A compact, horrifying and compelling story" *The Times*

HarperCollins *Children's Books*

Dear Olly,

Matt wouldn't look at her as he spoke.
"I'm going to be a clown, Olly, I mean a real clown.
And now I know where I'm going to do it.
I'm going where my swallows go. I'm going to Africa."

As Olly waits for her brother's letters, she watches the swallows preparing to leave for the winter. Hero the swallow starts his long journey to Africa, not knowing the terrible dangers he will meet on the way. And when Matt sees the children in the African orphanage – sick, injured and lonely – he knows he's made the right decisions, but he never could have dreamt of what was going to happen to him there…

"My daughter got to Michael Morpurgo's *Dear Olly* before me. 'This is excellent,' she informed me gravely. And it is… we both cried buckets." *The Times*

HarperCollins *Children's Books*

By Michael Morpurgo

The Amazing Story of Adolphus Tips
Private Peaceful
Cool!
The Dancing Bear
Farm Boy
Dear Olly
Billy the Kid
Toro! Toro!
The Butterfly Lion

For Younger Readers

Mr Skip
Jigger's Day Off

Picture Books

The Gentle Giant
Wombat Goes Walkabout

Audio

The Amazing Story of Adolphus Tips (read by Jenny Agutter and Michael Morpurgo)
Private Peaceful (read by Paul McGann)
Kensuke's Kingdom (read by Derek Jacobi)
Dear Olly (read by Paul McGann)
Out of the Ashes (read by Sophie Aldred)
The Butterfly Lion (read by Virginia McKenna and Michael Morpurgo)
Billy the Kid (read by Richard Attenborough)
Farm Boy (read by Derek Jacobi and Michael Morpurgo)